# Ever After High™ Epic Winter

## Royally Cool Adventure

Adapted by Perdita Finn

Based on the screenplay written by
Nina Bargiel, Sherry Klein, MJ Offen,
Audu Paden, and Keith Wagner

LITTLE, BROWN & COMPANY
LB kids

© 2016 Mattel, Inc. All rights reserved. EVER AFTER HIGH and associated trademarks are owned by and used under license from Mattel, Inc.

Little, Brown and Company

Hachette Book Group
1290 Avenue of the Americas, New York, NY 10104
Visit us at lb-kids.com

Little, Brown and Company is a division of Hachette Book Group, Inc. The Little, Brown name and logo are trademarks of Hachette Book Group, Inc.

The publisher is not responsible for websites (or their content) that are not owned by the publisher.

First Edition: November 2016

ISBN 978-0-316-35677-0

Library of Congress Control Number: 2016945004

10 9 8 7 6 5 4 3 2 1

CW

Printed in the United States of America

The Snow King and the Snow Queen gazed happily at their frosty kingdom.

"Let's play some indoor ice hockey," called their daughter, Crystal Winter.

"I'm up for that!" exclaimed the Snow King.

Crystal asked the palace pixies to help her lace up her skates.

Her mother shook her head. "If you're going to rule one day, it's high time you lace your own skates."

"C'mon, Mom, it's game time!" Crystal laughed.

Jackie Frost watched the family playing together. "Overgrown royal penguins," she muttered. Jackie didn't like the royal family. She wanted to rule the season—and the kingdom—herself.

"We need to turn the sweet Snow King sour," she told her brother, Northwind. "Then he'll start the most Wicked Winter ever after. Crystal isn't ready to rule, and she won't be able to take the heat. So once she's out of the picture, we save the day, and, before you know it, the season will belong to *me*!"

Jackie scattered a dark-pink dust over the king and queen. Evil was in the air! Crystal's parents rubbed their eyes. They looked around—and everything looked wrong. They frowned. They scowled.

Jackie clapped her hands. The curse was working!

The Snow King glared at his daughter. "You're acting like a spoiled brat!" he said angrily.

A moment later, he turned his wife into an ice sculpture. "Who else wants to play freeze tag?" He cackled. A speck of evil purple glinted in his eye.

Crystal was shocked by her father's sudden change in temperature. Something was fairy wrong! She needed her friends. It was time to travel to a land not so-far, far away.

"Ever After High, here I come!"

But at Ever After High, things were just as frosty.

*"Brrrr."* Briar Beauty shivered. "Did you feel that?"

"It just got freezing in here," Ashlynn Ella agreed. It was starting to snow!

Then the girls realized what was happening. Their friend Crystal Winter was back—and she had brought winter with her! It was the first summer snow day at Ever After High!

Most of the students loved the surprise snow day, but Daring Charming wasn't one of them. He also was upset because he had failed as Apple White's prince. He looked at his handsome reflection in a patch of shiny ice.

Daring's friend Rosabella Beauty had some advice for him. "Snow White's Prince Charming was bold, heroic, and selfless. Maybe it would help if you thought about helping somebody."

"Oh, I'm sorry," Daring replied. "I got distracted. What were you talking about? Something about me, right?"

Rosabella shook her head.

The Snow King had followed his daughter to Ever After High.

Daring was making a snow sculpture of himself when the king arrived. The Snow King ordered Daring to take care of his sleigh.

"Can't you see I'm busy?" Daring answered.

The Snow King flew into a rage. "Do I have to *spell* it out for you?" He blasted magic at Daring and stormed into the castle.

Daring felt a little funny. And then fur sprouted on the back of his neck….

"Blondie Lockes, reporting live outside Ever After High, where the weather is just *so* not right! And if the storm outside wasn't bad enough, it's twice as bad inside!"

Crystal knew she had to stop her father. He was unleashing the snowstorm of the century on Ever After High. Crystal and her friends made a plan.

Baba Yaga had seen the purple shard of evil in the Snow King's eye, so she knew why he was acting like he had such a cold heart. But the only counter curse was in an ancient scroll of deep magic in the Library of Elders—and the library had been destroyed a thousand years ago!

Then Farrah Goodfairy had an idea! She would use her fairy powers to glamour it back into existence so Crystal and her friends could find the scroll!

They searched through the Library of Elders and found the scroll hidden deep inside. *"Only the bouquet of the four Royal Roses of the Seasons has the power to undo the Kindness Blindness curse."*

"Talk about a strong perfume," said Briar.

*"Spring's Rose stands out, all alone. Summer's Rose wears a disguise. The Rose of Fall hides in the crowd. The Rose of Winter's found inside."*

Each Royal Rose of the Season was hidden in a different fairytale castle.

Blondie grinned. "You know what this means? Road trip!"

Crystal, Briar, Ashlynn, Rosabella, Blondie, and Faybelle set out to find the roses. On their way out of the castle, they ran into Daring… but he didn't look like himself.

"I'm a beast! My life is over!" wailed Daring in beast form.

Rosabella looked at Daring. "Hey, why don't you come with us? We're looking for a cure to a curse."

"You had me at *cure to a curse*." Daring grinned.

Jackie and Northwind weren't about to let Crystal and her friends reverse the curse! They turned themselves into snowy owls and followed their sleigh.

First stop was Rosabella's castle—where her father, the Beast, had given her mother a magic rose. But the rose bush wasn't in bloom. They would have to wait until spring…which the cursed Snow King would keep from coming. They were doomed!

Until Faybelle stepped forward. "Two, four, six, eight. Roses, bloom, we cannot wait. Winter, spring, summer, fall. Bloom till we can't count them all!"

The whole garden filled with blooming roses!

"Booyah!" shouted Faybelle.

On the way to Ashlynn's castle, the group got lost in a blinding blizzard.

"Where are we, Crystal?" asked Ashlynn, trying to hide her panic.

But Crystal didn't know. "My MirrorPhone is getting no bars. We're out of range."

Daring the Beast's nose twitched. He sniffed the air. He sneezed. "I can't even smell which way to go. My nose is full of icicles!"

Jackie and Northwind appeared in the woods. At first the friends thought the siblings were there to help them, but then they realized that the duo was there to start an avalanche!

Jackie laughed at Crystal. "You're even easier to fool than your dad!"

"Surprise!" added Northwind. "We put the curse on him!"

Jackie and Northwind flew away as a wall of snow buried the sleigh.

The group dug themselves out. A huge wall of snow blocked their way. But nothing was going to stop Crystal now. She had to rescue her family. Crystal made steps out of icicles so they could all climb up the wall. They could do this! One by one, they clambered to the top.

They had to find Cinderella's Rose of Summer—but it wasn't in her shoe closet where she kept her treasures. The scroll had said *Summer's Rose wears a disguise*. The friends realized it must be a riddle. So where was the rose hidden?

Ashlynn spotted the enchanted pumpkin, and Faybelle worked her magic on it. It was a really a secret greenhouse—and the rose was blooming right in the middle of it!

It was time to head to Briar's family castle—the home of Sleeping Beauty. The castle was covered in thousands of beautiful roses and every rose was covered in ice.

But Crystal suspected the magic rose was enchanted, and the most enchanted item in the whole castle was…the spinning wheel! Crystal began turning the spindle. Round and round it went—but it wasn't spinning thread; it was creating a glowing, magical yellow rose!

Blondie gasped. "Newsflash! This just in! We've found the Rose of Fall!"

The friends had found three roses, but the wickedest winter on record was growing wilder. They bravely went on! Their sleigh was headed into the heart of the storm—to Crystal's castle—to look for the Rose of Winter.

"We have to remove the curse from Crystal's parents," Briar exclaimed.

"And save the world of Ever After from eternal winter!" shouted Crystal.

Northwind was waiting for them in the castle. He had turned himself into an ice giant. "Turn back, by order of the new queen of winter, my sister, Jackie."

Daring the Beast wasn't scared. "I got this," he said.

"Crystal, run!" urged Rosabella. "Daring and I will handle this. I don't know how, but somehow we've got this!"

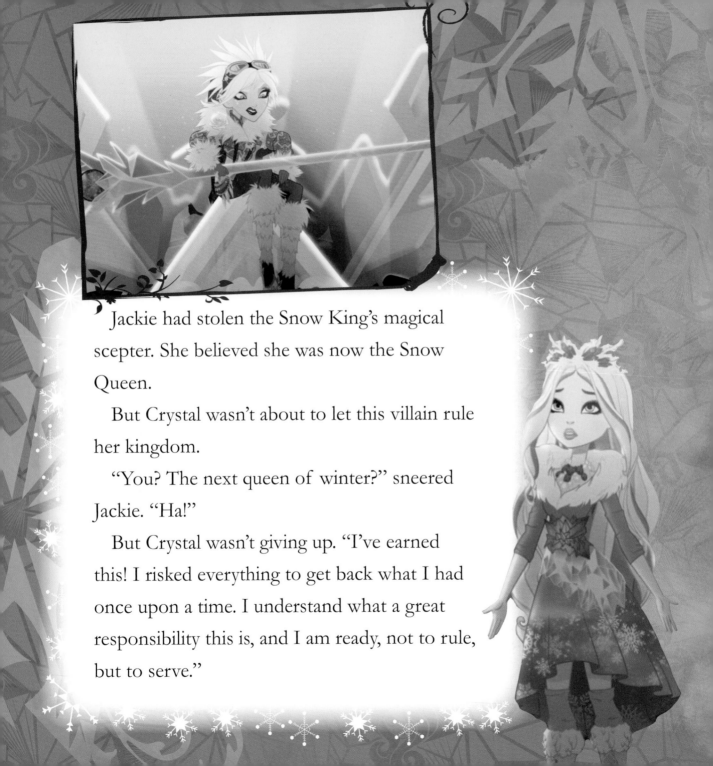

Jackie had stolen the Snow King's magical scepter. She believed she was now the Snow Queen.

But Crystal wasn't about to let this villain rule her kingdom.

"You? The next queen of winter?" sneered Jackie. "Ha!"

But Crystal wasn't giving up. "I've earned this! I risked everything to get back what I had once upon a time. I understand what a great responsibility this is, and I am ready, not to rule, but to serve."

Meanwhile, Daring and Rosabella figured out how to stop Northwind. They played a trick on him! They dared him to turn into a mouse…and he did! Daring realized that the most powerful magic of all was thinking of others. Rosabella had helped him learn this important lesson. Daring realized then whose prince he really was: Rosabella's.

Crystal used her ice hockey skills to defeat Jackie, sliding her right into a hockey net.

"Goal!" shouted Blondie. "What an upset!"

"You get to stay there until you learn to chillax," Crystal told Jackie.

The girls brought the four magic roses to the frozen king and queen. Crystal lifted the curse on her parents, and proved that she was ready to rule the kingdom of Winter. Her father gave her his scepter.

Crystal raised her hands. "I declare this a day of celebration, a day of fun, a…"

"*Snow day!*" shouted her friends.